Jesse Hodgson

Pip and the Bamboo Path

Flying E

High up in the Himalayan mountains lived
a little red panda and her mother.
Here, the trees grew tall and the roots ran deep.

But the tall trees were soon torn
down and their deep roots torn up!

"It's far too dangerous to stay here much longer,"
warned Pip's mother.

"But where will we make our nest now?" Pip worried.
"Without the trees we're lost."

Suddenly a bird swooped down and called out,
"You must find the bamboo path on the other side of the mountains.
It connects all the forests together and will lead you to safety."

Following the bird's lead,
they set off on their own
path into the Himalayas.
Together they trekked
through the mountains,
looking high and low
for the bamboo path.

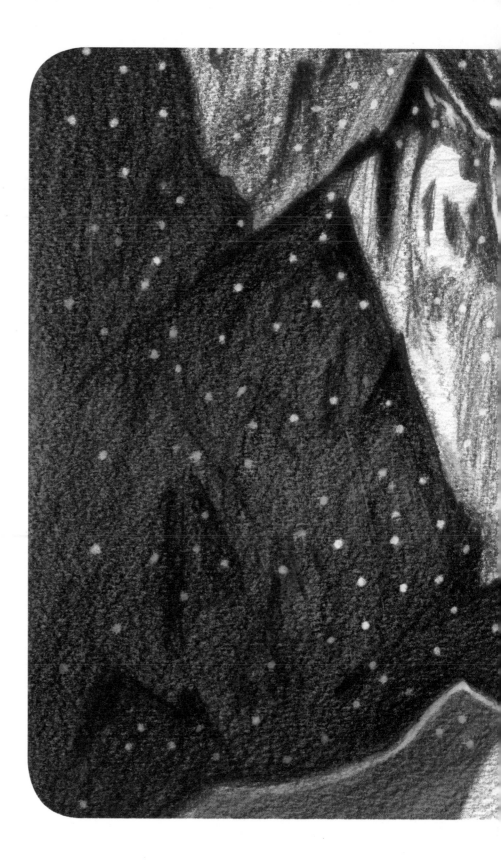

"Will it be on the other side?"
Pip asked.

As they climbed higher and higher it became colder and colder.
Spooky shadows crept up ahead.

"Can't we make our new nest here?"
a very scared Pip begged her mother.

"We must find the bamboo path," her mother
gently reminded Pip, as they kept moving.

After a while, they came
to the top of a rocky ravine.
"It's very steep," thought Pip.
"What could be down in those
cracks and crevices?"

They clambered on down the ledge, looking high and low for the bamboo path. The earth was too dusty and dry, and there were no fresh leaves for them to eat.

"Can't we stop here for a bit?" Pip yawned.
"This could be a good spot for our new nest."

"Not yet," said her mother.
"We need to keep searching for the bamboo path."

Soon they came to the edge of a city
with bright lights and busy streets.
Pip had never seen anything like it before.

Pip didn't like it here at all and in the chaos of the city, they lost their way.
They had travelled for a long time now and were feeling very tired.

"We'll have to make our nest here,"
sighed her mother.

"Somehow we'll survive on the city streets."

They were about to give up, when Pip spotted a firefly...

...and another, and another...

On the outskirts of the city, plants were still growing.
Her mother smiled, there was hope yet.

The fireflies led them to the bamboo path!
"The new forest can't be far away now," thought Pip.

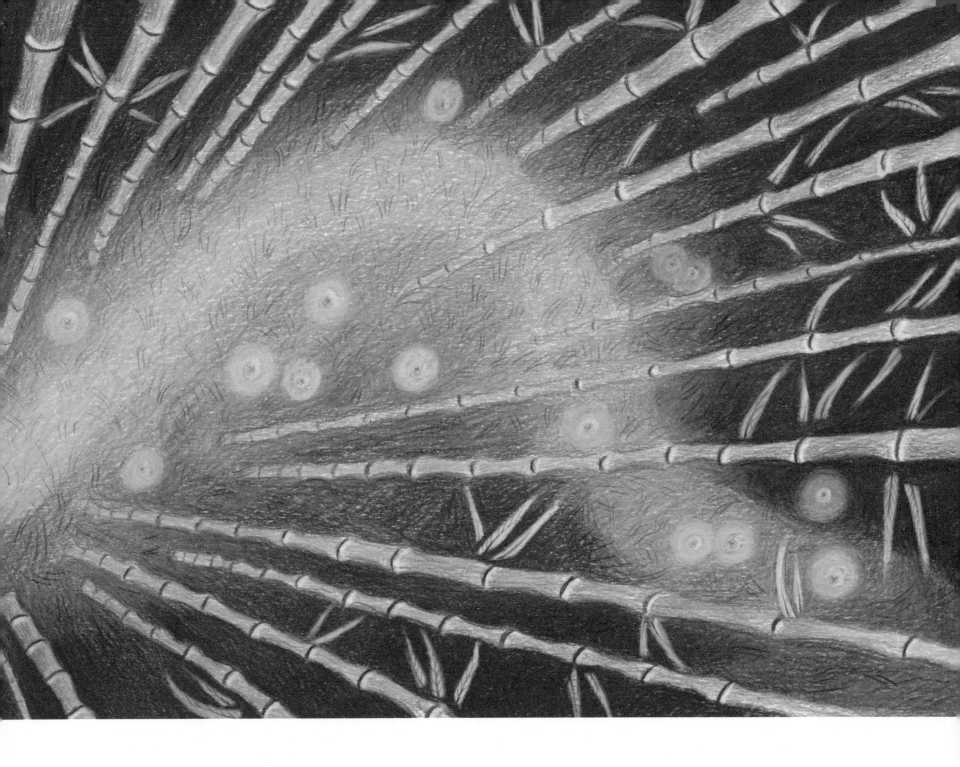

They followed the winding passage until
they found themselves among lush, tall trees.

All kinds of animals had come here from all over the Himalayas
in search of a safe place to make their home.

"Let's make our new nest here," said Pip.
And with a big yawn and a stretch…

...she curled up against her mother
and closed her eyes.

With the smallest seed of hope and a great deal
of courage, the little red pandas were home.

For my family

Pip and the Bamboo Path is © Flying Eye Books 2019

This is a first edition published in 2019 by Flying Eye Books,
an imprint of Nobrow Ltd. 27 Westgate Street, London E8 3RL

Text and illustrations © Jesse Hodgson 2019
Jesse has asserted her right under the Copyright, Designs and Patents Act,
1988, to be identified as the Author and Illustrator of this Work.

Published in the US by Nobrow (US) Inc.
Printed in Poland on FSC® certified paper.

ISBN: 978-1-911171-46-1
Order from www.flyingeyebooks.com